SINCE
LULU
LEARNED THE
CANCAN

By
OREL ODINOV
PROTOPOPESCU

ILLUSTRATIONS BY
SANDRA FORREST

GREEN TIGER PRESS

Published by Simon & Schuster

New York · London · Toronto · Sydney · Tokyo · Singapore

GREEN TIGER PRESS
Simon & Schuster Building
Rockefeller Center
1230 Avenue of the Americas
New York, New York, 10020
GREEN TIGER PRESS is an imprint of
Simon & Schuster Inc.
Designed by Sandra Forrest
Manufactured in the United States of America
10 9 8 7 6 5 4 3 2 1

Library of Congress Cataloging-in-Publication Data.
Protopopescu, Orel Odinov. Since Lulu learned the cancan /
Orel Odinov Protopopescu; illustrated by Sandra Forrest.
p. cm. Summary: A young ostrich does the cancan in every
imaginable place, sometimes to her family's dismay, and
sometimes to their advantage. [1. Ostriches—Fiction. 2.
Dancing—Fiction. 3. Stories in rhyme.] I. Forrest, Sandra,
ill. II. Title. PZ8.3.P937Si 1991 [E]—dc20 90-85014
ISBN 0-671-74791-6

To Nuria
—O.P.

For Steve
—S.F.

Since Lulu learned the cancan,
Our family's not the same.
She saw an old French movie
And we're sure that it's to blame.

SHE DANCES WHILE SHE'S SLEEPING.

THERE'S NO REST FROM HER STOMPING.

SHE PRANCES WHILE SHE'S EATING

IN RHYTHM WITH HER CHOMPING!

Grandpa Max can't play his sax
Without Lulu's ruffles showing.
She kicked a note and made it flat
But he just kept on blowing.

SHE DOES IT WITHOUT STOPPING.

SHE BOUNCES RIGHT THROUGH SCHOOL.

SHE GETS HER KICKS WHILE SHOPPING
AND ALSO IN THE POOL!

Brother Wayne worked on his plane
From Christmas to July.
He thought the thing would never go
Till Lulu made it fly!

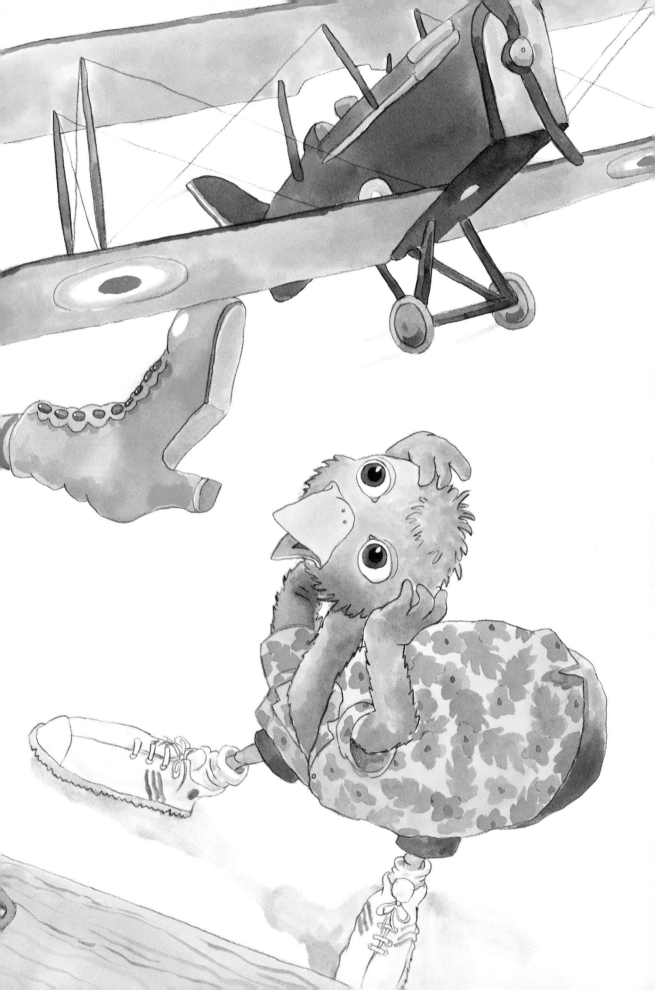

SHE DID IT AT THE EXHIBIT.

SHE CAPERED THROUGH THE PARK.

ON TABLETOPS SHE DID IT

AND SOMETIMES IN THE DARK!

Sister Kate went on a date
With handsome Chance LaRue...
"Nothing can come between us,"
He said to Lulu's shoe!

SHE DID IT OSTRICH STYLE.

SHE LET LOOSE AT THE ZOO.

THE CROCODILE LOST HIS SMILE

BUT THE MONKEYS DID IT TOO!

As catcher in the little league,
Did Lulu care who won?

When the umpire called the batter out
She kicked up a home run!

SHE THUMPED THROUGH THE SCHOOL PLAY.

SHE CLUMPED IN THE CHOIR.

SHE JUMPED ON HER BIRTHDAY

UNTIL HER SLIP CAUGHT FIRE!

Mom and Dad got very mad
When Lulu broke the TV…
But sometimes good things
    come from bad
For now they read with me.

THOUGH SHE SHOCKS OUR PET RABBIT

AND MAKES OUR TURTLE RUN

SHE JUST CAN'T KICK THE HABIT.

SHE'S HAVING TOO MUCH FUN!

Still we're hoping something
Will cool my sister's heels,
Before she figures out ways
Of doing it on wheels!